# Oh Brother, Little Brother

by Candid Brandon    illustrated by Alexandra Tatu

To siblings everywhere young and old—love each other ALWAYS!

—Candid

# Little Brother, let's get dressed.

# Oh brother, Little Brother.

# Little Brother,
# let's brush your teeth.

Oh brother, Little Brother.

# Little Brother,
# let's comb your hair.

# Oh brother, Little Brother.

Little Brother,
let's play outside.

# Oh brother, Little Brother.

# Little Brother, let's pet the cat.

# Oh brother, Little Brother.

# Little Brother, let's eat a snack.

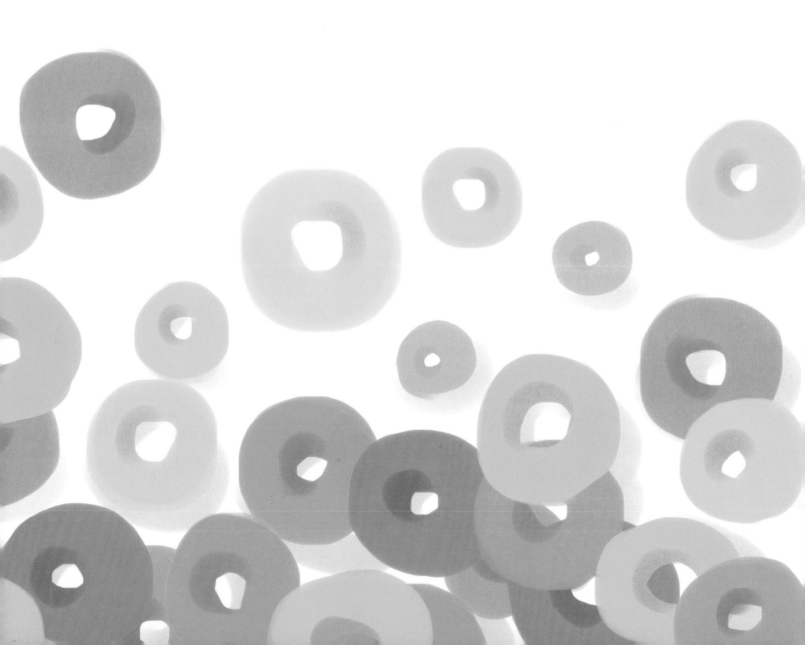

# Oh brother, Little Brother.

# Little Brother,
# let's play with toys.

# Oh brother, Little Brother.

Little Brother,
let's paint a picture.

# Oh brother, Little Brother.

# Little Brother, let's color the sky.

# Oh brother, Little Brother.

# Little Brother, let's clean up.

# Oh brother, Little Brother.

# Little Brother, let's read a book.

# Oh brother, Little Brother.

Little Brother,
let's take a nap.

Oh brother, Little Brother.

# Little Brother,
# you ruin everything!

# Oh brother, Little Brother, please don't cry.

# No matter what you do,

## I will always love you,
## Little Brother.

# Letter to the Grown-Ups

**Dear grown-ups,**

You may be wondering why this book is so repetitive. The reason is because this is a "predictable book." A predictable book is for young readers that uses rhyming and repetition of words, phrases, sentences, and events. Predictable stories are critical for reading development. Predictable books like *Oh Brother, Little Brother* use repetitive word patterns, familiar concepts, and simple story lines to make it easier for pre-readers and beginning readers to follow along. Children learn to anticipate words, phrases, or events when reading the story, and they will often participate in the reading.

*Oh Brother, Little Brother* was written to encourage pre-readers and beginning readers to read along with the repetitive word patterns and anticipate the shenanigans of the little brother. You might be asked to read this book over and over again, so here are some helpful tips for sharing this book:

- Allow time for the child to fill in the repeated phrase, "Oh brother, Little Brother."

- Encourage the child to repeat the phrase, "Oh brother, Little Brother."

- Allow time for the child to gather clues from the illustrations to fill in the big brother's suggestions, "Little Brother, let's…"

- Allow time for the child to predict what Little Brother will do next. Ask questions such as "What do *you* think Little Brother will do now?"

- Read *Oh Brother, Little Brother* over and over again to provide increased opportunities for the child to participate verbally.

- Read with inflection! Get into it and even use hand gestures.

- Point to the text as you read.

- Don't force reading. If the story isn't finished but the child wants to move on, then let the child move on. Encourage an attitude of joyful reading, not forced, resentful reading.

I hope you and your child or children enjoy reading this book as much as I enjoyed creating it.

**Candid**